Stories and rhymes in this book

Published by Ladybird Books Ltd
27 Wrights Lane London W8 5TZ
A Penguin Company
3 5 7 9 10 8 6 4 2

Produced for Ladybird Books Ltd by Nicola Baxter and Amanda Hawkes
The moral rights of the autor/illustrator have been asserted

Printed in Italy

The Creepy Crocodiles

by Irene Yates
illustrated by Martin Pierce

Ladybird

CROCS COME CREEPING
Here come the crocodiles,
Creeping in the park...
Creeping in the daytime,
And creeping in the dark.

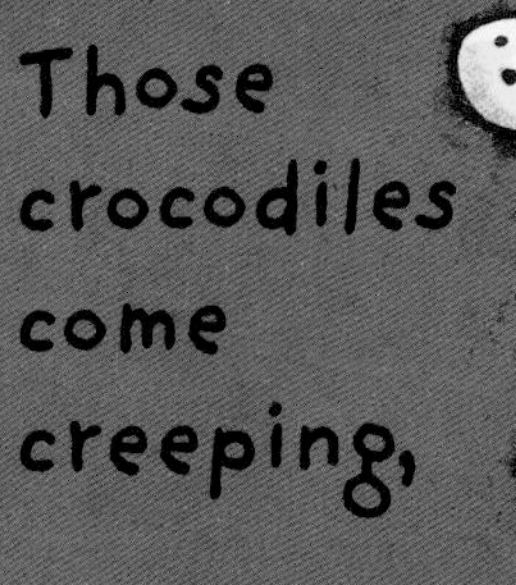

Those
crocodiles
come
creeping,

Come
creeping
everywhere,

Keep looking
right behind
you...

There might
be one just
THERE!

WATCH OUT... FOR THE CREEPY CROCODILES!

The Creepy Crocodiles are very big...

They have long, pointed snouts and enormous jaws...

with lots of pointy teeth that go...

SNAP, SNAP, **SNAP!**

The Creepy Crocodiles have two powerful arms...

and two even MORE powerful legs...

to help them creep along.

They have GIGANTIC tails that can thrash and thump... and swish... and swing.

And they have two beady eyes on top of their heads.

The Creepy Crocodiles live
in Town Centre Park.
But don't worry...

Although
they creep...
and creep...
and creep...

they move
so slowly,
they fall
asleep!

PLAYING IN THE PARK

Watch out by the roundabout!
Be careful on the swings!
Always check the climbing
frame...

For very CREEPY things!

SEE C. C. C.
Meet Calvin Creepy Crocodile. He thinks he's a really COOL croc.
Off he goes... creep, creep, creep... on the look-out for dinner.

He looks on the water
for dippy ducks drifting
and diving.

He looks under the water
for fat fish flashing by.

He looks along the river bank for bunnies bouncing,

And while he's looking out, Calvin Creepy Crocodile is floating along the river, pretending to be a log.

He thinks he's **SO COOL!**

The trouble with Calvin is, he's so cool that the ducks dabble right over him...

fat fish flash right past him...

bunnies
bounce,

snakes slither

and lizards lounge without
noticing him at all.

None of them are even a tiny bit scared of Calvin Creepy Crocodile...

because they all know that
when he's being cool, he
falls fast asleep!

TIME FOR TEA

Whatever you do,
Don't ever invite
A Creepy Crocodile
Round for a bite.

He might sit on the sofa
And watch your TV,

Then gobble you up
As a snack for his tea!

FORTY WINKS

Grandma Creepy Crocodile is very old and very wrinkly!

She's so old that all her teeth have fallen out...

and she wears a set of dentures.

Every time Grandma Creepy Crocodile opens her enormous jaws to go
SNAP,
SNAP,
SNAP...

her false teeth go
CLICK, CLICK, CLICK...
(and sometimes they fall out!)

This morning, Grandma is creeping about, thinking about breakfast.

The Park Keeper opens the park gates.

In come the
boys and girls
to play.
In come the
mums to show
off their
babies...
and the
dads for a
nice little
snooze.

And along comes Grandma Creepy Crocodile.

She opens her huge jaws to give everyone a fright.

But all they hear are her false teeth going CLICK, CLICK, CLICK...

and no one
is frightened
at all.

"Never mind, I'll have
forty winks instead," says
Grandma. SSNNORRE!

BEWARE!
Creepy Crocs
Have lots of teeth.
They're sharp at the top
And sharp underneath.
When they
open their
mouths wide,
To give you
a grin,

You have to watch out
That they don't...

Pop you IN!

A LITTLE NAP

Mum Creepy Crocodile's ten toddlers are playing her up...

swishing each other with their tails.

"STOP SWISHING TAILS!"
she cries.
But the creepy toddlers
take no notice.

SNAP!
SNAP!
SNAP!
The toddlers go to each other.

"STOP SNAPPING!"
cries Mum Creepy Crocodile.
But the creepy toddlers
don't listen.

They just want to play
on the swings and the
roundabout and the slide.

"OH, NO YOU DON'T!" cries Mum. But before she can stop them, they're off!

They're creeping and crawling up the river bank...

and across
the grass...
and over
to the
playground.
"OH!" cry
the children
in the
playground...

"The Creepy Crocodile toddlers are SO CUTE!"

They pick them up and cuddle them.

They sing them nursery rhymes.

They take
them on the
swings...
and the
roundabout...
and
the slide.

And Mum Creepy Crocodile thinks, “Well, I’ll just let them play for five minutes.”

But before long, Mum Creepy Crocodile is doing what crocodiles do best!

CROCODILE FOOD
Crocs aren't keen on apples.
They're not too fond of peas.
I'm afraid they spit out cornflakes.
And they can't stand cheese.

Soup has a habit of spilling.
It leaks through the gaps in their teeth.

And they just hate greens,
Spaghetti and beans

(Though some like the toast underneath).

No, what Creepy Crocodiles LOVE to eat...

is MEAT!